Forever My Valentine

Written By KT Loomis

AuthorHouse™
1663 Liberty Drive
Bloomington, IN 47403
www.authorhouse.com
Phone: 1 (800) 839-8640

Published by AuthorHouse 03/28/2019

ISBN: 978-1-7283-0558-5 (sc)
ISBN: 978-1-7283-0557-8 (e)

Library of Congress Control Number: 2019903485

Print information available on the last page.

authorHOUSE®

To Mikayla, without you in my life
my heart would still be broken.
And to my family and friends, thank
you for all of your support and love.

Once upon a time in a village outside
Okinawa, Japan, lived a young girl who was
known throughout the village as Valentine.

She had the appearance of a girl around the age of 12, but those old enough knew better. They knew her appearance was misleading since this child had a heart and mind much older than her looks.

She was known for bravery, kindness, wisdom and her pure nature.

She was outrageously smart and all
her friends loved when she told stories,
especially her best friend Katarzyna.

Only those closest to her knew of her powers. She could eat a whole bag of cheese sticks in 2 seconds...

shoot a soccer ball from midfield and
take out the goalie while scoring...

If these powers weren't enough, she had one more that's so outrageous that most people can't believe it!

Valentine has the ability to give someone a heart! I know, how is this possible?!?

No one knows. Not even Valentine.

It all started when Valentine, an orphan, was found on the footsteps of a hospital. That same morning there was a young lady in the hospital with her, sharing the same room.

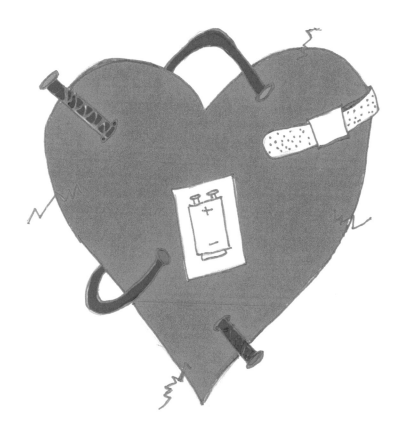

This young lady had been in a horrible accident that left her with a broken heart.

Lonely and scared, this young lady asked if she could hold Valentine and sing to her throughout the day.

The doctors agreed to let the young lady hold Valentine. This began their remarkable tale.

As the days and nights passed on something uncanny was happening to the young lady's heart.

Incredibly, it was the relationship between Valentine and this young lady that gave her a healthy heart.

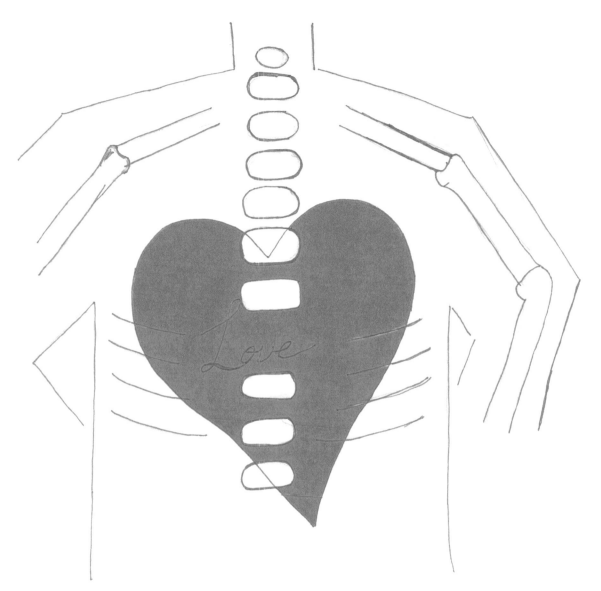

Valentine gave her a heart, but NOT just any heart, a heart filled with love, a very powerful substance.

Soon the young lady was well enough to leave the hospital, but before she left she adopted Valentine.

To this day, the young lady's heart is stronger than it ever was before and it's all because of Valentine.

The End.

Author Biography

KT Loomis lives in Germany with her partner and their daughter. Her passion for books turned an assignment to parents from her daughter's 7th grade teachers into Forever My Valentine. Becoming a mother at the age of 18, she is aware of the complex and beautiful gift of motherhood. In this, her first publication, she reveals a piece of her own journey in learning to embrace the gift. Her daughter's love of anime inspired the setting and made it a collaborative effort. Writing has now become a creative outlet for her and a medium for teaching, another of her passions.

Printed in the United States
By Bookmasters